The Liberty Boys Running the Blockade; or, Getting Out of New York

Harry Moore

THE LIBERTY BOYS OF 76

A Weekly Magazine containing Stories of the American Revolution.

FRANK TOUSEY, PUBLISHER, 168 WEST 23D STREET, NEW YORK

No. 1110   NEW YORK, APRIL 7, 1922   Price 7 Cents

The redcoats and the nightwatch pursued Dick to the very edge of the wharf. The boat containing the Liberty Boys was just putting out. Dick jumped and was caught by Harry. The redcoats were too late

CHAPTER I.–A Clever Capture.

"I think that fellow is following us, Bob."

"What fellow, Dick?"

"The one on the other side of the way, the man with a beard and a steeple-crowned hat."

"Yes, I see him, but why should he follow us, Dick?"

"To obtain information, I suppose. He is certainly watching and following us and if we were to stop anywhere you would see that he would do the same."

"Suppose we try it, Dick?"

"Very well. I may get some information myself. There is Fraunces' tavern. That is as good as any place."

"Yes, for that is a general resort for army officers, and if this man is a spy, as you seem to think, he will be very likely to go to just such places."

The boys, well built and handsome, bronzed from exposure to the weather and wearing the uniform of the Continental army, were making their way along Wall street in the City of New York one pleasant September afternoon. Dick Slater was the captain and Bob Estabrook the first lieutenant of the Liberty Boys, a band of one hundred sterling young patriots engaged in the war for American independence, and at that time quartered in New York, on the Commons at the upper end of town.

As they were walking along Wall street, Dick, who was very observant, noticed a man on the opposite side of the street, who seemed to be watching them closely as if with an idea of learning what they knew, and following them wherever they went. At this time the city was threatened by the British, who held Long Island and had ships at Staten Island just across from Manhattan ready to proceed up the rivers at any time. The presence of British spies in the city was suspected, and Dick, who was an expert spy himself, had his suspicions concerning the man opposite as soon as he saw the fellow.

Turning into Broad Street, the boys walked down and at once the spy, if he were one, took the same direction. Fraunces tavern, on the corner of Broad and Pearl streets, was at that time a great resort for army officers and men-about-town, and was, therefore, just the place which the boys would frequent. Crossing the street when they reached Pearl street, the boys went into the tavern, and were shortly followed by the man in the steeple-crowned hat, who took a seat at a table near enough to understand all that they said.

Giving Bob a wink, Dick began talking about some supposed exploit with some one in the army, and went on from that to telling of meeting certain beautiful young ladies, and how the latter were so charmed with him and other boastful talk. The man was evidently greatly disgusted at having to listen to such talk, as he had evidently expected to hear something different, and he shortly moved his seat to another part of the room.

"He had no interest in hearing how Polly Perkins winked at you, Dick," laughed Bob.

"No, but he wants to find out more about us, nevertheless. Don't look over there. He has a very pretty scheme, I can see."

The man was drinking strong ale from a pewter and, having finished it, set the pewter down. Dick saw him scratch something on it and beckon almost imperceptably to a man near by who had just entered. Then, as if by accident, knocked his pewter off the table to the floor. The other man came forward, picked it up and set it on the table, but Dick could see that he glanced at it at the same time, and then, as if upon a place to sit, came toward them and sat three or four tables away. The suspected spy presently arose and went out and Dick said:

"Well, good-by, Bob. I will meet you at Trinity church in half an hour."

Then muttering the words, "Bowling Green, ten minutes," he walked away, going past the table where the man with the steeple-crowned hat had been sitting and carelessly knocking off the pewter. Picking it up, he looked at it and saw scratched on one side: "Follow Slater."

"So, this is another, as I supposed," he thought. "There are several spies in town, and they know me and are trying either to learn something or to get possession of me. We shall have to turn the tables on them."

He made his way to the Bowling Green, meeting on the way four or five of the Liberty Boys.

"Go up to Trinity church, boys," he said, "stroll about the place carelessly. There is British spy watching my movements and I wish to watch him and, if possible, to catch him. The man is short and rather stout and had a red face. There is another, who may not join him at once, who wears a black suit and a steeple-crowned hat and has a beard. He will send the other one first, I think."

"All right, Captain," replied the boy, whose name was Ben Spurlock. "We will watch him. Come along, Sam."

Dick had gone on, meanwhile, the boys proceeding in couples or singly to the church, where they scattered about waiting further instructions from the young captain. Bob appeared at the Bowling Green at the appointed time, and said:

"The fellow was cautious and did not follow me, but I suppose he will be at the church."

"Probably, as his instructions were to follow me. Did he stay as long as you did?"

"Yes, and remained after I left. You will see him at the church, no doubt. The other man may be there. Come into the nearest tavern and exchange coats with me. We will see if these men are observant or not."

"Very good," laughed Bob.

In the private bar of the tavern the boys were alone long enough to make the exchange, and then Dick sent Bob ahead and told him to wait in the churchyard for him or some one wearing his own uniform.

"You are the captain now, Bob," with a laugh, "but I don't know who will be the lieutenant yet. That will depend."

Dick then went over to Stone street, where he entered a little shop kept by a draper, to whom he said:

"I want an ordinary suit of clothes, Mr. Towns. I am watching a spy and I think it just as well not to be in uniform."

"I see, Captain. You are wearing the lieutenant's coat now."

"You are very observant," smiling. "I will leave it here and send one of the boys for it."

"Very good, Captain. Step into the wareroom and take what you wish."

The wareroom was no bigger than the shop, but the different suits were hanging about the sides, and Dick quickly selected one not likely to attract much attention, and put it on, leaving the uniform behind. On Whitehall street Dick met one of the boys, Phil Waters by name, and directed him to go to the draper's and put on Bob's coat over his own, the young lieutenant being of a heavier build. As Phil did not have his musket with him, the change was easily effected, and no one not knowing him would suspect that he was not the lieutenant.

"Go and meet Bob," Dick said, "and talk about anything but matters of importance. Do not recognize me and watch the man whom you see observing you and Bob."

"All right, Captain," and Phil went away to make the change.

Then Dick took his way up to the church and waited for the spy to appear. Coming out of the church after a stay of a few minutes, Dick saw Bob in the yard, standing contemplating a monument, while not far away stood the second spy watching him. At the time mentioned, Phil, who was supposed to be Bob, came up, and the two began to chat in the most animated fashion. Dick saw the spy approach them so as to overhear their conversation, and at once signaled to Ben, Sam, Harry, Will and others whom he saw in the grounds to approach rapidly.

Bob and Phil were talking away in the liveliest fashion about all sorts of things except matters of importance, the spy standing behind a monument listening to them and trying to discover what connection the talk had with the situation in the city. Dick meanwhile had gathered the various groups together, and they were now closing in upon the spy, ready to act as soon as they got the word from the captain. The man with the steeple-crowned hat was not to be seen, and Dick was uncertain whether to wait for him or not. Then the spy stepped up to Bob and Phil and said glibly:

"Good day, Captain. You don't remember me, I suppose? I met you on Long Island. So you are over here now? Where is your camp? I should like to send up an ox or two for your use. Where did you say you were encamped?"

Dick passed at that moment but was not observed, nor was a certain sign he made to Bob. Then the call of a bird was heard and Ben, Sam and the rest began to close in.

"On the Commons," replied Bob. "Come up and see us some time. You are Mr. Bulwinkle, are you not?"

"Yes. I see you remember me very well."

Then all at once he found himself surrounded by Liberty Boys, and a young man in plain garments stepped up and said:

"You are a British spy. You and a man in a steeple-crowned hat in Fraunces tavern tried to listen to my conversation. I have not yet caught your employer, but if you make any alarm or try to get away you will be denounced. Go with these boys. They will show you our camp, where you will remain a prisoner until I can deliver you up to General Putnam."

The man's face blanched, and then he recognized Dick, and muttered:

"Jove! you are Slater, the rebel, himself! How did you manage—"

"Slater, the patriot, you mean. Your superior is not very clever. I detected him following us. Then he sat too close. Next he scratched a message on the pewter after beckoning to you. You were told to follow me. You thought I was coming here in uniform, didn't you? After practically telling you that I was going to be here. I am afraid you are new at spying, too. Go with the boys, but talk and laugh and don't let any one think that you are a prisoner."

"Jove! but I never would have suspected you of all this clever work." muttered the other.

"I did not want you to!" laughed Dick and he and Bob went one way, while the boys went another with their prisoner.

CHAPTER II.–The Spy in Danger.

Dick Slater and Bob Estabrook set off down Broadway and had nearly reached Bowling Green when Dick saw the man in the steeple-crowned hat approaching. He evidently took Dick for his friend at first, for he came forward quickly, and then suddenly stopped, looked at both boys, flushed, and, turning upon his heel, darted across Broadway and into Pearl street, where he disappeared. Dick was after him at once, but by the time he reached Pearl street, nothing was to be seen of the spy.

The boys walked down to Whitehall wharf, where they could see over to Staten Island, where the British ships seemed to be getting ready to change their positions. The day was wearing on rapidly, and as they could not get any additional information at the wharf, they turned their faces toward the city and made their way at a good jog toward the Commons, where the camp was located. As they neared Thames street, above the church, Dick said in a low tone:

"There is that spy going down the street. He has changed his disguise and I would not be surprised if he had taken off his beard.

"Where is he, Dick?" eagerly.

"Going down Thames street on the right, the man in brown with a cocked hat. I recognize his walk. Keep behind him, Bob. The sight of a Continental uniform may have a bad effect upon him."

"But he has seen you in that disguise, Dick."

"Yes, and there is nothing striking about it. He would have to see my face to recognize me and I shall take care that he does not."

Indeed, Dick had so many ways of changing his expression, that it was quite likely he could deceive the spy even were they to meet face to face. Bob kept behind Dick as they went down the street on the same side as the spy, the young patriot watching the man closely, and at length seeing him go into a wine shop of a rather unsavory reputation. When he disappeared, Dick turned to Bob and said quickly:

"There is another door to this place down the alley. Go there at once and watch for this fellow to come out. He will do so as soon as he recognizes me."

Then Dick waited a moment for Bob to go down the alley, and entered the shop. He saw the spy sitting at a table, and now, having his own expression, was recognized in a moment.

"Good afternoon," he said, as he walked over to the spy, who was unable to repress a start of surprise. "You did not expect to see me here, did you?"

"Who are you?" the other snarled. "I don't know you from a side of sole leather. Why do you speak to me?"

"I am Captain Dick Slater," said Dick, taking a seat opposite the spy. "You escaped me just now and changed your dress and also took off your beard. You had a friend–a short, somewhat stout man. We have taken care of him. You will find my lieutenant at the other door. I see you are looking toward it. I think you had better go out that way. Time presses, and we had better go now."

The spy suddenly arose, started for the door, threw the chair in front of Dick and shouted:

"This boy is a British spy! Hold him while I go for the guard!"

Then he flew toward the door and was out of it. At once the men in the shop began surging toward Dick with evil looks on their faces, and some drawing ugly-looking knives.

"That is the cry of 'Stop, thief!' to draw attention from himself," said Dick. "My gentleman is a spy himself. I am Dick Slater, captain of the Liberty Boys. I think you may have heard of me. Don't be afraid. My lieutenant is at the other door."

Then, quickly pushing the chair aside Dick left by the door he had entered and then around to the alley. The spy had evidently thought that Dick was deceiving him, but as he went into the alley he saw Bob, who quickly caught him by the arm and said:

"Wait a moment. The captain will be out in a second and will want to see you. There is no such haste."

Then Dick came down the alley, and Bob said with a careless laugh and a quizzical expression:

"Here is the captain. I have his uniform, but he is the captain, just the same."

The spy got up, glared at Dick and said angrily:

"You are making a great fuss over nothing. I am not a spy, as you think. I am an attorney and have—"

"Why did you try to escape, why did you call me a spy, why did you change your clothes, why did you follow me into Frances tavern, why did you instruct your companion to follow me, if you are not a spy? Attorneys don't do these things."

The man turned sallow, smiled in a sickly fashion, and said:

"This was all to test you. General Putnam had his doubts as to your efficiency and wished me to put you to the—"

The boys laughed at this flimsy excuse, and Dick said shortly:

"You will go with us. I am well acquainted with General Putnam, who is in command in the city. You know that, of course. We will go to his quarters now."

The man suddenly thrust his hand into his pocket and withdrew a packet, which he tried to throw over a fence, but was prevented by Bob.

"You had better give that to me," he said, taking the packet and putting it in his own pocket.

"Come!" said Dick. "It is nearly sunset. If you attempt any more nonsense I shall call the guard. You know me, and you know why you are arrested, and you are simply trying to throw obstacles in my way and so make your escape."

The spy made no reply, and remained quiet for the rest of their way to the general's quarters. Leaving the prisoner under guard, Dick shortly saw the general himself and related what had occurred.

"H'm! spies in the city, eh?" muttered the veteran. "This is an important capture, Captain. I must compliment you on a very pretty piece of work. I shall have to see this man."

Dick had the packet which Bob had taken from the spy, and he gave it to the general, while the man was being sent for. Putnam looked it over and said:

"This proves conclusively that the man is a spy. You have the other one, you say, Captain?"

"Yes, in our camp. I can deliver him to-night or in the morning, as you please."

"I think it had better be to-night," shortly.

"Very well," and at that moment the spy was ushered into the general's presence, turning pale as he saw the veteran and realized what his fate would be. Dick then took his leave and he and Bob returned with all speed to the camp.

CHAPTER III.–In the Stone House.

Reaching the camp, the boys were heartily welcomed by the Liberty Boys, who knew that something had happened when Ben and the rest came in with a prisoner and were eager to hear the rest.

"Did you get the other fellow, Captain?" asked Sam.

"Yes, and we left him holding an interview with General Putnam."

"In which he was likely to get the worst of the argument," put in Ben dryly.

At that moment a jolly-looking Irish boy up and said, giving a comical salute:

"Captain dear, supper do be ready an' the young leddies have come to camp, an' will ye ate thim foirst–Oi mane mate thim foirst an' ate supper afther, or phwativer?"

There was a laugh, and then two young very pretty young ladies rode up to the fire and were helped to dismount by Dick and Bob. The girls were their sisters and their sweethearts also, the sister of each being the sweetheart of the other, and were as constant companions as the boys themselves. They lived in Westchester county and had come to visit friends in New York, stopping on the way to see the boys.

"Well, Alice," said Dick to his sweetheart, "so you have come to the city, have you? Things are in a rather turbulent state, but I fancy we can get you out of it in case there is any immediate trouble. You will stay to supper, of course. Patsy has just announced that it is ready, so we will lose no time in sitting down."

The girls were well known to all the Liberty Boys and when they sat down they received a general salute, every boy there being glad to see them. After supper the boys who had brought in the spy took him to the general's quarters, and shortly after this Dick and Bob set out with the girls to see them to the house of their friends in the city. Dick and Bob took their horses, the captain riding a magnificent black Arabian and Bob a fine bay, and all set out together, laughing and talking in lively fashion. They struck across the Common to the road running to the west of it, and would then make their way into the city past the new church and Broadway to Maiden Lane.

As they were going on at an easy jog, expecting to leave the Common, four or five dark forms suddenly sprang up in front of them and seize their bridles, while as many ran up behind and prevented their wheeling. Then some one flashed the light of a lantern in their faces, and a voice was heard saying:

"H'm! women! We don't want them. All want is the rebels!"

The girls' horses were at once set free, and the girls themselves lost no time in wheeling and dashing back toward the camp, Alice taking the lead.

"Hi! what are you doing?" growled one of men, who were all evil-looking fellows, as Dick could see. "The gals will bring the rest of the rebels."

Dick was dragged from the back of Major, his black Arabian, and one of the men attempted to mount the animal to go in chase of the two girls but was immediately thrown.

"Back to camp, Major!" said Dick.

In an instant the intelligent animal was flying after the girls, who quickly recognized his hoof-beats. Meanwhile the men who had captured Dick and Bob knew the danger they would run remaining on the ground, and they hurried away with the two boys, letting Bob's bay go free. They went on so rapidly that Dick was unable to see much of the way, but he knew the direction they took almost by instinct, and could have returned without trouble if he had been liberated. The men kept the two boys in the middle of the party and held on to them tightly.

"We got the rebels an' we'll get the reward," said one.

"Yes, the gals an' the other rebels won't be able to find the house, and they can hunt all they like."

It was a sharp decline to the river, down the lane, and one of the men stumbled and rolled several yards, picking himself up with a grunt and a groan and a lot of bad language, and then hurrying after the rest. Dick heard the swash of the water on the gravel bank, and then saw the river itself dimly, but in another moment some dark object loomed up before him, and then he and Bob were taken into a house, the front of which was much lower than the back on account of the steepness of the hank. The boys were taken to the front and then down a flight of steps to a room in the rear, where they were left in the dark, the door being locked and barred on the outside.

"Who are these fellows, do you suppose, Dick?" asked Bob, when they were left alone.

"I don't know. Tories, no doubt, or just men who want the reward offered for my capture."

"But there is none offered for me," with a laugh. "Why should they take me with them?"

"To keep you from giving the alarm. They would have taken the girls if they had thought twice."

"But will the girls be able to show them the way?"

"They can take them to where we were attacked, and after that the boys will follow the trail. Mark is a good hand at that sort of thing, and he will have good boys to help him."

"Yes, they would all turn out and join in the hunt if he asked them," declared Bob.

"But there is no use in our staying in the dark, Bob," said Dick. "You have matches with you?"

"Yes. They did not search us and I have matches, and my pistols and everything."

Bob then lighted a sulphur match, the only kind in use at the time, and looked about him. They were in a room with one door but no windows, and were evidently under guard at the back of the stone house. Dick listened attentively for some minutes, and at last heard the sound of some one coming downstairs.

"Put out the light, Bob," he said, in a low tone. "If they see it under the door they may get suspicious."

Bob blew out the candle, and in a moment all was dark and still in the room.

"When the door opens make a rush at it, Bob, and overturn the fellows. There are two of them."

Bob stood ready to act upon the instant, and the steps of the two men coming on could be heard plainer than ever, rays of light beginning to show under the door. The men said nothing, and came on softly, but Dick's ears were very sharp, and he could hear them with no trouble.

The key was turned in the lock and the bolts shot back, and then, as the door opened slowly, the boys both threw their weight upon it suddenly and sent it flying wide open in an instant. There was a startled cry and a heavy fall, and in a moment the place was thrown into profound darkness.

"Pick them up and lock them in, Bob," said Dick, and the boys hurried into the passage, presently stumbling upon two men who were just getting upon their feet.

They seized the men, threw them into the room, closed the door and locked them in, taking out the key, and then looked for the lantern as they heard a call from above.

CHAPTER IV.–The Boys' Escape.

"Hallo, down there, what's the matter?" called some one at the head of the stairs.

"The blame rebels tried to get out and upset the lantern," answered Dick, in a gruff voice.

"Huh! where are they now?"

"They're all right. We locked the door again."

"H'm! we better come down and help you. We gotter take them away."

"All right, come on, an' fetch another light."

Then the boys began to move steadily toward the stairs, finally finding them.

"Come on, Bob," whispered Dick. "Don't waste any ceremony on them, but tumble them downstairs as soon as they come. They won't get the others out in a hurry, for I have the key."

The boys went rapidly upstairs, but, just as a light appeared at the top, the men in the room below began to shout:

"Hallo! Bill, Toby, look out for them rebels; they've shut us up in the storeroom!"

"Hurry, Bob!" hissed Dick.

The two boys dashed up to the top of the steps and came upon two men carrying lanterns. In an instant each seized one of the Tories and sent him rolling down the stairs uttering startled yells. Then they hurried forward in the dark to the front of the stone house, opened the door and ran out. At the same moment they heard shouts from the house, and then shots were fired, the bullets passing over their heads. They returned the shots, and heard a yell, and a sudden slamming of a door, and then a cry from up the bank:

"Hallo! Dick, Bob, are you there?"

"Yes, Mark, coming right along!" shouted Dick, and then he and Bob hurried up the steep bank, presently seeing lanterns and a number of the Liberty Boys.

"We had some little trouble in finding the place," declared Mark, when Dick and Bob joined him and the rest, there being fully a score of them. "The young ladies had no idea where the wretches had gone, but we picked up the trail at length and then had less difficulty in following it. Where were you?"

"In the stone house–a regular nest of thieves," Dick answered. "I must have a look at the place later."

There was no further sound from below, and the boys went on to the top, where they found several of the Liberty Boys and the two girls.

Dick and Bob now jumped into the saddle and resumed their interrupted ride, going with the girls to the house in Maiden Lane. The friends of Alice and Edith were very charming girls, and the boys spent an hour or two very pleasantly, telling the story of their adventures in the afternoon and evening, and talking of the situation in in the city. The boys at length left the house to return to the camp, Alice and Edith expressing considerable anxiety, however, lest they be way-laid by the men who had already made an unsuccessful attempt to keep them prisoners.

In a short time they were back in camp, the occasional tramp of a sentry or the sudden flaring up of a fire from a puff of night air being the only things to show that there was any one there. The Liberty Boys were always vigilant, for one never knew when an enemy might be about, and Dick had taught them to be on the lookout at all times, whether they expected a foe or not. After breakfast Dick took a party of about a dozen of the boys in addition to Bob, and set out for the stone house on the river. Reaching the lane, the boys dismounted, the descent being rather too steep for the horses, and Dick, Bob and seven or eight others went down. The door toward the road was closed and there was no sign of life about the place. Dick and Bob went down to the shore where there was a little wharf, and here they found a door on the lower story, this being closed, however, as were the windows, and no one stirring either in or about the house.

"The place looks like an ordinary storehouse," remarked Dick, "and I suppose that the people about here think it is such. I shall have to get permission from the general to examine it, for it is a nest of thieves whatever else it may be."

"That is plain enough!" muttered Bob.

Taking Bob, and leaving the boys to watch the place, Dick set out for Putnam's headquarters to report concerning the place and ask what should be done. Some of the boys remained on the bank above, and some on the wharf and near the lower door. They found a passage under the wharf, and then another dug through the earth, and leading to a door evidently in the stone house under the bank and back of the wharf.

"These fellows are regular smugglers as well as thieves!" exclaimed Harry. "This is an important discovery. They use this place to take in stolen goods when they are afraid to take them in any other, I guess."

"See if the door is locked," suggested Sam.

Then he and Harry tried it, and found that it was not fastened, but opened readily when they lifted the latch.

"Hallo! Who is there?" cried a gruff voice, as they advanced.

"Here's one of the rascals! Catch him!" cried Harry.

CHAPTER V.–An Important Capture.

Dick and Bob set out upon their horses for the general's quarters, and upon reaching Broadway met the girls coming along on horseback.

"I am afraid we cannot give you much attention now, girls," said Dick. "We are going to the general's quarters, and then to rout out the thieves, who make a rendezvous of the stone house and I think we shall be very busy for sometime."

"You might go up to the camp and cheer Patsy's heart by a visit," laughed Bob. "He is fond of the girls."

"You want us to get the poor boy in trouble, I see," said Alice. "You would get so jealous that Patsy would have no peace."

"You know what Carl says when he disagrees with any one, don't you, Sis?" asked Bob, with a sly wink.

"Come, my dear," replied Alice. "I think we shall be able to do without their company for a time. We ought to be resourceful enough for that."

"But, Alice, brother and Bob have business to attend to, and—"

"And you are a dear little matter of face goose and can't see a joke," laughed Alice. "You would spoil both those boys, but it needs me to put them in the right place."

Then the girls rode away toward the camp, while the boys went on to the general's. The veteran listened to Dick, and said:

"By all means break into the place and make a thorough investigation, Captain. If there is any complaint, say that I gave you full authority to act. There is something very about the whole affair, and I do not believe that the place is used for honest purposes."

"Nor we, General, but we wanted your authority before we proceeded to vigorous measures."

"Well, you have it now, Captain," said the general, who was well acquainted with Dick, Bob and many of the Liberty Boys.

They left the place, jumped into the saddle, were going up toward the Commons when, as they neared the head of Maiden Lane, they suddenly heard a sharp cry, and saw a young girl in a chaise come dashing toward them at a terrific pace, the horse having taken fright at something and being now beyond the girl's control.

"Quick, Bob!" cried Dick. "We must save her!"

"Why, it's Sarah Watrous," said Bob, that being the name of the girls' friend whom the boys had seen the night before.

The boys dashed forward, one on each side the chaise, Dick dismounting and catching of the bridle, throwing himself backward and checking the animal's speed. Bob reached out at the same time and did what he could to stop horse, the two boys between them succeeding in checking him in a short time.

"Oh, I am so glad you came!" gasped the girl who seemed nearly ready to swoon. "I don't know what I should have done without you. He never ran away before and I didn't know what do."

"What started him up, Miss Watrous?" asked Dick, stroking the horse and getting him into calmer mood.

"I am sure I don't know. I have been before and he never acted in this fashion."

"Who harnessed him?" asked Bob, looking the horse.

"Why, I did. The boy was busy and I couldn't wait, so I did it myself. Why shouldn't I do things for myself instead of being always dependent upon others?"

"That is all right in theory," laughed Bob, "but you have not done it right, and the horse has been chafed and annoyed, and has finally tried to get out of it and has run away. You had better let me fix things."

"Well, I declare!" exclaimed the girl. "And I thought I could do most anything!"

Just then Dick caught sight of one of the men he had seen the night before going down Broadway, and he said to Bob in a low tone:

"Look after the young lady, Bob. There is one of those ruffians. Take Major up with you when you get through."

Then he went away at not too rapid a walk and followed the man he had seen, observing him go into a tavern on the other side of the street and just below the corner.

"Not a very reputable place," he said to himself, "but I think I am safe enough."

Entering the place, he saw the man he had followed sitting in a corner talking to a man who, if he was not greatly mistaken, was the chief of the two spies he had captured the day before and had turned over to General Putnam. The man recognized him, and hastily arose, and Dick knew that he was not mistaken, although how he should have escaped was a puzzle to him.

"Stop that man! He is a spy of the British!" he cried. "And the man with him is a thief!"

"Better not talk too loud in this place, you saucy young rebel!" growled the landlord, coming forward. "All my customers are respectable persons, and if you don't like 'em, your room is preferable to your company."

From the black looks cast at him, Dick saw that he was likely to get into trouble, the patrons of the place being evidently persons of shady character and Tories. He pushed forward, nevertheless, and, suddenly drawing a pistol, said in a very determined manner:

"If you attempt to stop me you do it at your own risk. One of those men is an enemy to the country and the other an enemy to society, and I purpose to arrest them both."

"Run, Hughson!" muttered the thief. "I'll fix the young rebel. He threw me downstairs last night, and—"

Dick sprang upon the table, leaped to the floor, seized the thief by the collar and dragged him to the door, and then, turning upon the men in the place, said:

"If any one attempts to follow he will get hurt, so I advise you to remain where you are!"

Then, dragging the man out of the door, he said:

"The spy can wait. I have got you and you will have to give an account of yourself. Keep quiet, or I will hand you over to the bailiffs at once. You must know by this time that I am a boy of considerable determination."

They were in the alley by this time, and Dick, with his hand on the man's collar, continued:

"Will you go along quietly or shall I call a constable?"

"H'm! you've got more pluck than a dozen constables!" the fellow growled. "Oh, I'll go along with you, 'cause you've got the best o' me. You didn't get Hughson, anyhow. How did you know I was with him?"

"I did not, but I knew you and was determined to have you. You can give me some information concerning the stone house, and later I will look after the spy."

The man gave a grunt, and by that time they were out upon a side street leading into Broadway or to the river.

"We will go there now," said Dick. "Some of the Liberty Boys are waiting for me at the house and we can continue our investigations with your assistance."

"Huh! you seem to think I am going to tell you all I know about the place," muttered the man. "S'pose I don't?"

"Then you will get into worse trouble," shortly.

It was dark in the room, so the boys could not see the man who had challenged them, their matches having burned out: Harry stumbled over something on the floor and fell headlong, Sam falling on top of him. At the same instant came a flash and a report, and the boys saw the man about to make a dash for the door. Will lighted another match, and Harry and Sam managed to scramble to their feet, but were not quick enough to intercept the man, who made a sudden spring, dashed Will aside, and was out into the passage.

"After him!" cried the boys in unison.

But that was a difficult matter, for the passage, like the room, was cluttered with packages and bundles of various sizes. They could hear the sound of his footsteps, but could catch no glimpse of him, nor could they tell which way he had gone, for passages seemed to open on both sides.

"H'm! I'm afraid we've lost him!" exclaimed Will, as they came to a standstill in the dark. "I wish we had a better light than these matches give. It's impossible to chase around here in the dark among all these boxes and packages, and with passages leading every which way."

"Listen!" exclaimed Harry. "There's some one coming this way."

There was the sound of more than one man coming toward them from the river side of the house.

"We might better conceal ourselves," whispered Will.

The three boys quickly drew to one side, and feeling a barrel standing near the wall, one dropped behind it, while another hid behind a box, and the other concealed himself in an angle of the wall. The sounds did not proceed from the passage through which the three boys had just passed, but from one on the right side, and seemed to come from more than one person and who were trying to proceed quietly, evidently with the intention of keeping their presence unknown as long as possible.

"They must be somewhere about here," they heard some one whisper. "We must never let them get away."

Then suddenly a lantern flashed its light over their heads, and they heard the words:

"Well, they're not here, at any rate."

The steps passed their hiding places, and the boys decided that there were three men.

"If we could meet them on our own ground, we'd be more than a match for them," muttered Harry. "But this strange place and in the dark, we'd be completely at their mercy."

"Yes, and with the other rascal lurking about," answered Sam.

Just then they heard a long, shrill, peculiar whistle. The boys started, for they did not recognize it. Following almost immediately came the report of fire arms.

"Come along, boys!" cried Harry. "There's something doing somewhere, and we must be on the spot!"

They all rushed on blindly in the dark, following the direction whence the shot proceeded, the way still as dark as Erebus, but seemingly straight ahead. When Dick and his partner reached the stone house on the river, the man would have passed the door, but Dick held him back, saying sharply:

"I know the house. I want to save time by having you show me its secret passages and explain what nefarious practices are being carried on in the place."

The man made no reply, but walked up the steps to the front door, opened it with a key, and then passed into the unlighted hall, into which the daylight could not penetrate, on account of the solid wooden door shutting it off from the street, and the doors into the rooms all being closed. A sudden misgiving seized Dick. Had he been prudent in coming into this strange house alone with an avowed enemy? It was true the Liberty Boys were somewhere about, but could they reach him in time, should danger present itself? He drew out both pistols, and backed against the wall, while he made the man procure a light. Instead he gave a long shrill whistle, which was immediately answered, and there could be heard the onrushing of feet. The Tory gave a mocking laugh, exclaiming:

"Captain Slater of the Liberty Boys has walked into his own trap!"

The only reply Dick made was to give the melancholy hoot of an owl. The prisoner jumped and looked about, and then laughed a little sheepishly, but at the same instant, there came bursting into the hallway the three ruffians who had passed the other boys such a short time before.

"Surrender!" hissed the Tory.

CHAPTER VI.–In Dangerous Quarters.

"Not at all!" cried Dick, pistols in hand and barring the passage of the three men. "Stop where you are! Hallo, boys!"

"All right, Captain, here we are!" shouted Sam and Harry.

"Sure we'll be with ye in a minyute, Captain dear!" answered the Irish Liberty Boy.

"Off dere was some fighding been we was dere already pooty quick, I bet me!" laughed Carl.

"Who is in a trap now?" asked Dick, with a laugh.

Then the five Liberty Boys suddenly dashed up and leaped upon the smugglers or Tories, whichever they were. In a moment they were disarmed, Dick putting his pistol to his prisoners head and saying sternly:

"Now perhaps you will tell me what I want to know. You men are thieves, smugglers, Tories, aren't you?"

"We make our money with as little trouble as possible," the man replied.

"And you have helped spies of the enemy to get information?"

"For pay, yes. Hughson would have paid us well if we could have delivered you to him."

"Take these fellows to Putnam's quarters, boys," said Dick. "He will know how to deal with them. Patsy, get me a torch or a lantern."

"Sure there do be wan just beyant, Captain. Wan o' thim rapscallions dhropped it. Oi'll have it for ye in a minyute."

Sam and the others marched the prisoners away, and then Patsy came with the lantern as Bob arrived, having taken Sarah Watrous part of the way to the camp, where she would join Alice and Edith.

"Hallo! You have a prisoner, eh?" said Bob.

"Yes, and he is going to show us all over this place."

The fellow had no means of escape now, and Dick's pistol at his head made him do what he would not have done under other circumstances. The place had been a warehouse, but was supposed to be closed, the gang of thieves and smugglers having used it for some months free from discovery, bringing and taking things from it at night and evading discovery all that time.

There were other warehouses and storehouses along the river, and a few houses, but the men had worked so quietly, most of the time entering by way of the river that no one knew of their being around. There was considerable plunder in the house at this time, and Dick meant to find owners for it if possible, and if not, to offer it at public sale and use the money thus obtained to further the cause of independence. Pike was greatly chagrined at being forced to show Dick about, and said gruffly:

"Well, you rebels have got the best of us, but you won't enjoy it long. When Howe gets hold of your city, as he will before many days, you will have to leave."

"But by that time you will have been hanged as a spy and a thief and will know nothing about it," replied Dick.

"H'm! Hughson got away and so will I," boastfully.

"I shall see to it that you do not," shortly.

Having finished the examination of the stone house, Dick took Pike to the general's headquarters and turned him over, the man being put under guard at once and some men sent to watch the place.

Hughson had escaped through the negligence of a fresh recruit, who had not understood the importance of his prisoner, and had supposed him to be simply a man who had been locked up for insubordination and was sorry for it, Hughson carrying the thing through cleverly.

"The man will be more careful the next time, having been so close to punishment," thought Dick, "and knowing that we are in earnest and will show him no mercy."

Dick went one way and Bob another, both in disguise, for the very sight of a Continental uniform would frighten the man now and put him on his guard. Dick made his way along the wharves on both rivers, keeping a lookout for the man, but without success, seeing many suspicious characters, but none whom he knew to be spies. Having settled the business, he went to the camp, where he found the girls and Sarah Watrous being entertained by the Liberty Boys.

After dinner the girls returned alone, Dick being busy looking for signs of the enemy along shore, and going around the city in disguise searching for the spy, who he believed would try to learn more about the disposition of the troops on the island, the forts, the amount of supplies, the roads and other matters of importance. It was getting on toward evening, and Dick was over on the East River side of the city, when he saw a boy of about fourteen being abused by an evil-looking man.

"What are you striking that boy for?" he asked, stepping up and putting the boy behind him.

"I got a right to abuse him, he's mine!" snarled the other. "The ungrateful hound won't do things for his own dad."

"Is this man your father?" Dick asked.

"Yes, he is, but I don't want to give him the money I earn to buy drink with, for then he abuses mother and the little children and —"

"Haven't I got a right to the money he makes?" growled the man.

"Not to misuse," retorted Dick quickly. "The boy is right in protecting his mother, and if he can do it by withholding money to be used in buying strong drink which takes away your reason, he has a right to do so. Why don't you go to work?"

"You better mind your own business!" with a snarl. "I am a gentleman and wasn't brought up to work."

"The greater misfortune!" shortly. "If you had known the dignity of labor, you would not be the wretched man you are now. Go to work and stop making a beast of yourself, or you may end your days on the gallows or in a prison."

"If he don't give it to me now, I'll get it out of him another time," the man growled. "I've a right to the money, and I'll flay him alive if I don't get it!"

"If I hear of your harming the boy I'll have you sent to jail," said Dick decidedly. "Run home, boy, and give the money to your mother. If this man troubles you or your mother, go and tell General Putnam, and we will see that the offence is not repeated."

"We'll see whether you will or not!" hissed the man, suddenly flying at Dick as if to annihilate him.

In a moment Dick was on the defensive, and, then, taking the offensive, sent the man rolling into the gutter.

"There! Perhaps you think I can do as I say now!" he said. "Keep on with your abuse of your wife and family and you will catch it still worse. A word to the wise is sufficient."

The boy ran away, quickly disappearing down a narrow street, while the man, getting on his feet, glared at Dick and said:

The Liberty Boys Running the Blockade

"You're a rebel, that's what you are, and all the rebels will be driven out'n this town, and then we gentlemen can do as we like."

"You gentlemen may be in jail or hanged by that time, and so know nothing about it," dryly. "You are a pretty sort of gentlemen! I'd rather not be one if you are a good specimen."

"I'll keep you in mind, my fine fellow," with a snarl. "You don't strike me for nothing, let me tell you that!"

"I did not I struck you for a good reason, and whenever the occasion rises again I will do the same, and you may remember that!" and then Dick turned on his heel and walked away, having caught sight of a man whom he had seen on the other side of the city, and whom he suspected to be one of Hughson's cronies, having seen him in the tavern near the Bowling Green. He followed the man carelessly so as to avoid suspicion, and presently saw him go into a low groggery down the street. The boy's father stood watching Dick for a time and then went off, Dick following the man he had seen and paying no attention to the other. He found the fellow sitting on a bench with others, but kept out of sight as much as possible, not knowing if he would be recognized.

"Been drove out of our place over on t'other side of the city, hain't you, Jeb?" asked one.

"Yes, by a lot of confounded rebels, too, and just as we was getting ready to sell off a lot of the stuff," snarled the other. "I'd like to get hold of the fellows!"

"Maybe when the redcoats come in you will, unless they get scared and get out before that."

"Yes, maybe. Seen Hughson over this way? He had a narrow shave of it. Come 'most to stretching a rope for old Put. Them same young rebels caught him."

30

"No, I ain't seen him, but I heard he was looking around to find all he could about the rebels so as to give the general a better show for getting in. Light up here, Jim, it's getting dark."

A hulking-looking man in a corner now arose to get lights, as it was growing dark in the place, and at the same moment some one entered and said:

"They've got Pike hard and fast, and Wendell was hanged this morning. I'd like to get hold of Slater and some of his—hello!"

The big man came along with a lantern, and Hughson, for it was the spy himself, suddenly caught sight of Dick and recognized him.

"What's the matter?" tried several of the men in the place, leaping to their feet.

"There's the rebel now–Slater himself!" cried Hughson. "Don't let him get away! The boy in the brown homespun suit!"

In an instant a rush was made for Dick.

CHAPTER VII.–An Act of Gratitude.

Seeing his danger, Dick whipped out a pistol and shot the lantern out of the big man's hand, making a sudden dash for the door. As he reached it, however, some one came in, there was a collision and Dick and the newcomer fell to the floor with a crash.

"Hallo! can't you see where you're going?" the fellow yelled, and Dick recognized his voice as that of the man who had been, abusing the boy farther up the street.

The spy, Jeb and others now rushed forward, lights were procured and Dick was surrounded and made a prisoner.

"H'm! that's the rebel that said I shouldn't spend my own boy's money," the newcomer muttered. "I owe him a grudge and I'll pay it, too. No rebel strikes me for nothing!"

"You know him, do you, Fletch?" asked Hughson.

"Yes, I know him. I didn't know he was Dick Slater, but I know him, and I've got a grudge against him and I'm going to settle it. You was counting on taking him to the general, I suppose?"

"Yes, but get him out of the way. Some one might come in."

Dick was taken into a rear room where there was not much light and bound hand and foot. At length he heard footsteps in the passage outside, and then the door was opened and two men came in, followed by a boy carrying a lantern in his hand. The men picked Dick up and carried him out, but not before he had seen the boy's face, and the boy had seen him and had given him a swift look of intelligence. The boy was the one he had befriended, and however he happened to be here, whether he was leagued with these evil men or not, Dick knew that he would help him. The boy went ahead, down a flight of stairs to a damp cellar, and along a passage to some place where there was a damp smell and foul odors from the swamps along the river.

"Set him down, Bill," said one of the men, and Dick was placed on the ground on his back.

"Go after the bag, Tom," one man said, "or send your pop and the rest here."

"Won't do it!" said the boy. "Dad will beat me. Go yourself. I will watch him."

"Go on, Jeb."

"Go yourself, or come along. Tom ain't used to these things, and the old man will lick him, too. Knows you're here, does he, boy?"

"No, he don't. Safest place for me is the grog shop when he has no money, 'cause he won't come there."

"He'll be here all right, then," with a laugh. "He wouldn't miss seein' the rebel chucked into the water. Come on, Bill. Here, give us your lantern, Tom."

"All right," and Dick knew by the gathering shadows that the men were going away.

Then the boy suddenly kneeled at his side and said in a hoarse whisper and with great excitement:

"I found out where you was, Captain, and made up my mind to save you. I've got a knife and will cut the ropes. Wish I had the lantern. Never mind, I can feel. Can you roll over?"

"Yes, I guess so," but at that moment there were other footsteps and more lights and hoarse voices.

"Never mind, Captain, I'll do it yet!" hissed the boy. "I'll do it if I have to kill dad and the lot of 'em."

Then the spy, the boy's father, the landlord, and the men who had brought Dick to the place, came up and the boy slunk back into the darkness and awaited his time.

"Got the bag there, Bill?"

"Yes; here it is."

Two of the men picked Dick up, while another held the sack open and drew it over his feet. The boy came up, and Dick felt a keen bladed knife put between his hands and for an instant saw the face of the boy.

"Here, get out of the way!"

"Hold him steady, Jeb!"

"Don't be so long there with that sack!"

"Hurry up, there, he's as heavy as lead!"

The sack was drawn up over Dick's head and tied tight with a stout rope, the men then carrying him between them to the end of the passage and up some steps. One or two tested the rope to see that it was all right and then the men holding Dick gave the sack a swing or two and cast it well out upon the water, where it struck with a splash and then sank. Dick could hold his breath for nearly two minutes and he knew that he would not need all that. While the men were swinging him he clutched the handle of the knife, turned the blade down and began to cut through the sack. When he began to sink he moved his hands toward his head and cut a straight gash in the sack. Then he moved his hands the other way and began to kick vigorously, so as to loosen the sack. Then, as he began to think he could hold his breath no longer, he felt himself rising, the sack fell away from him, and in a few moments he shot up to the surface alongside some huge object which he recognized as the hull of a vessel. Then he lay on his back and floated, and, holding the knife in his teeth, cut the cords that bound his wrists and his hands were free.

Swimming noiselessly alongside the vessel, which was anchored in the river, he reached the fore chains. He was now free to use both hands and feet, and the next thing to do was to get to shore. He had his knife which Tom had given him and this he resolved to keep till he was safely out of all his dangers. Making his way around the anchored vessel, he set out for shore, guided by the few lights along the water and in the taverns. Suddenly he heard the sound of oars and then of voices.

"How did he get hold of a knife?" asked Hughson.

"I dunno, but he'll have to float and we ought to find him," replied Jeb.

The sack had been drawn ashore, and the slash in it discovered and now the men were trying to find Dick. The boat was coming directly toward him, and in a few moments he could distinguish its outlines dimly and see the forms of three men in it rowing directly toward him. Then he sank well down and swam right under the boat, coming up a yard or so beyond it as it went on toward the middle of the river.

CHAPTER VIII.–Tom's Defiance.

"Hallo! there's some one swimming in the river!" cried the spy.

"So it is," growled Jeb. "Hello there!"

"Put about," muttered Fletch. "It's the rebel. He can float. We must get after him."

Dick swam on, the boat putting about, and now the light of a lantern was shining over the waters.

"Ha! there he is!"

"Shoot the rebel, no one will hear!"

"Yes, we've got to get him!"

Crack! There was a report, but Dick had just sunk under water and was unhurt. On came the boat, Dick rising just astern of it. In a moment he seized the gunwale and swung the boat around with all his might, at the same time tipping it at one side. There was a cry of alarm, and then some one cried from the ship Dick had seen:

"Get away from here, you water rats, or you'll get a shot or two in your gullets that you won't like."

There was a sudden splash, and Dick knew that some one had fallen into the river from the boat. He had released it, and was now making his way toward the wharf at good speed. There were more outcries from the river, but Dick could not see the lantern now, and judged that it had fallen overboard. The inability of the men to see Dick worked for his safety now, and he swam on to the wharf at a good rate. Nearing it, he heard the boy Tom say in a cautious voice:

"Who is that?"

"It is I, Tom, thanks to you," said Dick. "Without that knife I should have been drowned."

"Come this way, Captain," added the boy. "Do you see me?"

"No, but I know where you are."

Dick swam toward the boy and was helped by him to land.

"You saved me from a thrashing, and you saved the money I had for my mother," the boy said. "But for that he would have got it, and mother and the little children would have had nothing to eat."

"You earn money for your mother and the children, do you?" asked Dick, interested.

"Yes, sometimes quite a good deal, but I have to be careful about it, for if he finds out that I have it, he takes it away and then we have to go without. I have to lie to save it often. Is that very wicked, Captain?"

"No, it would be better for you not to lie, but to face him down and tell him plainly that the money was for the support of the family and not for him to squander in drink."

They were hurrying along now, the boy in the lead, the sounds from the river showing that the men were coming back.

"Yes, that is right and I shall do it, but come, they will raise an alarm and you will have trouble in getting away. This way, Captain."

They went down an alley, the boy taking Dick's hand, and presently turned into a narrower one where Tom shortly pushed open a door and entered a house.

"It is Tom, mother," the boy said. "I have got the captain with me. The scheme worked well, fortunately, and he cut his way through the sack."

"You were obliged to take desperate chances, sir," said a woman's voice, "and I told Tom that I feared they would be too desperate. He would have released you if he could."

"Yes, I know, ma'am, but he gave me great assistance and I am accustomed to taking desperate chances."

The woman lighted a tallow dip and then exclaimed in surprise:

"Why, Tom, you said he was a captain! This is but a boy, not very many years older than yourself."

"He is the captain of the Liberty Boys, mother. They are all boys, some of them no older than myself. This way, Captain, and I will get you some clothes to take the place of the wet ones."

The boy then led the way into a smaller room, where he brought out a suit of clothes somewhat small for Dick, but neat and clean.

"You had best keep them," said Dick, as he removed his soaking garments, "and if you will come to the camp to-morrow, you can have your own again."

He rapidly exchanged the wet for the dry clothes, Tom giving him a ruffled shirt, saying:

"That is a gentleman's shirt, but I suppose you do not mind, on a pinch?"

"No," with a laugh, "I do not, but I hear some one coming."

"Yes, but he does not know of this place, and if you are quiet he will not hear you. There is another way out which I will show you."

Dick finished his dressing as he heard Fletch say:

"Some one helped the rebel, and I'd like to catch him! Where is that boy Tom?"

"He is not here."

"Well, I can see that!" savagely. "Where is he?"

"He has gone out," simply.

"Whereabouts? To earn money? He gave you some to-night. Where is it?"

"You cannot have it," resolutely. "Some of it has been spent for the children and the rest is put away."

"I want it. I am drenched and chill with cold. The plagued rebel upset me into the river. I must have liquor to take out the chill. Give me the money."

"No, I will not. I will make you some hot tea, which will be better for you. I have never refused to help you when you were yourself, but I will not let you turn yourself into a beast and make the children go hungry and naked."

"Give me the money, I say!" savagely, and then Dick heard a frightened scream from the other room.

"Quick, let me out, Tom!" he cried.

The boy was ahead of him, but Dick followed only an instant behind, sprang into the room he had left and seized the angry, half-drunken man as he was about to throw the woman to the floor.

"Stop that, you brute, or you will get into a worse place than the river!" he cried. "Aren't you ashamed of yourself?"

He had thrown the man on the floor but he now got up and rushed at him, knife in hand. Dick had the knife which Tom had given him, and he met the other's attack resolutely. The two blades clashed together, and the man's knife fell to the floor, the boy picking it up.

39

"I told the captain I would kill you, if need be, to save him," he said, "and I'll do it all the quicker to save my mother. You are a miserable, drunken brute, not fit to live with decent folk. Go away, I will not have you here."

"You?" repeated the man shamefully. "What have you to do with it? Isn't this my house, aren't you my son, isn't your mother my wife? Where else should I go? How can you turn me out–you, a mere boy?"

"Because I am the breadwinner, because you are a drone, an idle, worthless fellow. You are not fit to associate with us. You are no father of mine; I disown you!"

"You cannot put me out," snarled the man, advancing.

"If he cannot, I can!" said Dick, with determination. "If you do not leave here at once, I will drag you out and denounce you as an associate of spies, an habitual drunkard and a thief. Are you going?"

"Yes," muttered the man, cowed by Dick's resolute bearing.

Then he went out, and Dick said in a low tone:

"He will not venture to return at once, but he will seek out his evil companions and try to overcome me yet. I must go. You are a brave boy, Tom. Stick to your mother above all others, and you will come out all right. Good-by, come and see us at the camp to-morrow."

Then Dick hurried out, and made his way toward Broadway where he would be safe. Reaching a main thoroughfare at length, he went on and at last entered the camp, where he was challenged by Ben Spurlock.

"Who goes there?" cried the boy.

"Captain Slater," was Dick's reply.

Then Ben gave a signal which brought a score of the boys running to the spot in an instant.

"Lieutenant Estabrook has gone out to look for you, Captain, and taken a strong party of the Liberty Boys," said Mark Morrison, coming forward. "Were you on the East River side of the city?"

"Yes, Lieutenant, and have had some very exciting adventures. Send some of the boys over toward the river, and I think they will find the others. Tell them I am all right."

The boys gave a cheer, and then Mark despatched a dozen boys to look for Bob, Dick going to his tent to change his clothes. In time Bob and his boys came back, and there was great rejoicing in camp, everybody being anxious to hear Dick's adventures. Dick told them, the boys being more incensed than ever at the spy and determined to capture him and put him out of the way of doing any more mischief.

"That boy Tom was a plucky fellow and a grateful one as well," declared Bob. "That is the sort we want in the Liberty Boys."

"Yes, but he is needed at home," Dick returned, "and would probably have to do the cause good in other ways than joining us. He would be an acquisition, of course, but I would not ask him."

All was quiet in camp at length, and no alarms of the approach of the enemy were heard, although it was not long before they would be.

CHAPTER IX.–The Spy in the Toils.

The next morning Tom came into camp, the boys giving him a hearty cheer as soon as they knew who he was, and asked to see Dick.

"He has not come back all night," he said, and Dick knew that he referred to his father. "I do not think he will return. He is afraid to come back. I shall be very glad to leave the city because I think I shall get more work outside and mother and the children will do much better."

"I think it will be better for you all," Dick returned. "If the enemy gets hold of the city there will be much suffering, I am afraid. If you leave you will avoid this. I can find you a place where there will be work enough for all, and where you will not be troubled by your father when he is in his cups."

"He is always in them of late years and has greatly changed toward mother and all of us. The little children are afraid of him and will not go near him, but I must protect my mother."

"That is right, Tom. Always do it. Perhaps if your father stopped his bad habits he would be better again, but it is best for you to go away from him entirely and live apart until you see what changes time may bring about."

"Yes, I think so, and I shall go as far away as I can and start for myself. You know some good place?"

"Yes, and I can put your mother and the little ones, with good people where they will be taken care of until you are established, and they can look out for themselves. We live in Westchester, about twenty miles away, which will be far enough to keep your father from finding you and not too far away to get plenty of work."

"I shall be very glad to go there," simply.

"My mother and sister and the lieutenant's parents and sister live there, besides many of the boys' families, and it will be no difficult matter to get you all the work you can do, and work for your mother as well. It will be a better place to live than the city, and you will be in no danger from your father."

"I would like a place like that," said Tom. "It would be better for all of us!"

"Then I will make arrangements for your mother and the children to go up there at once and you can follow shortly. The enemy will eventually get possession of the city, and you will be better off out of it than in it.

"I will get ready as soon as you say, Captain," shortly.

"Then I think you had better not delay, for I believe that it is a matter of a few days only, perhaps not more than one, when the enemy will be in possession."

The boy then went away, and in half an hour Alice and Edith came to the camp, and Dick told them about Tom and his mother.

"I think you had better return shortly, Alice," he added, "and take the boy's mother and the little children with you. Tom will very soon establish himself when he gets there and will be much better off than in New York."

The girls were ready to go very shortly, for the evidences of the enemy's preparations to seize the city were more and more visible. One or two ships had gone up the East River the previous night, and the ships were all much nearer to the city than they had been the day before. After Alice and Edith had gone, Dick and Bob went down to the lower end of the city to investigate, and found one or two ships at Governor's Island, just opposite, the people in the lower sections being in a state of considerable anxiety.

"That looks as if there might be something going on in a short time," muttered Bob.

"I think so myself, and I am glad that I suggested to the girls that they had better leave. The British are getting ready to invade the city, and we don't know how soon they may attack us on all sides."

"Then we will all have to get out or else be obliged to run the blockade."

"Exactly, and we must learn all we can of Howe's moves."

During the afternoon Tom came to the camp with his mother and the little children, reporting that his father had not been seen since the night before, and that he thought the man feared arrest and had fled or was in hiding in some of the lower quarters of the city. Dick obtained a horse and chaise to take the mother and children, Tom driving, being more or less used to horses. The two girls came in just as these preparations had been completed, and it was shortly after dinner that they all started on their way to White Plains.

They were all glad to get away, and Tom was particularly pleased at the prospect of getting his mother out of the city, where her health and that of the children would be greatly improved, and where they would all be free from the fear of the father. When they all set out, the boys gave them a hearty cheer, and Dick and Bob went away with them, intending to ride a few miles and take a look at the river on the way. The boys left him at the Greenwich village and then came back by the river road, in order to see whatever might be going on. They were something below the old village, when, nearing a tavern by the roadside, Dick reined in and said excitedly:

"There is that rascal now! I hope he has not seen us."

"Which rascal do you mean, Dick?" asked Bob, halting just behind Dick and looking around.

"Hughson, the spy. I did not see his face, but I know his figure. He is dressed as a drover and will probably go into the city, thinking that we do not know him."

"Was he at the inn, Dick?"

"Yes, drinking home-brew and smoking a long pipe, taking his comfort, evidently. As I saw his back only, it is not likely that he saw me."

"We ought to catch him, Dick."

"Yes, and this is a good place, as there are no Tories in the village, and the people of the inn will help us. Take the rear, Bob, and I will go to the front of the house."

The boys separated, Dick riding at once to the front door of the inn and dismounting. He saw the man at one of the windows and was sure of him. In a moment the fellow turned, saw Dick and started for the rear. As he was going out, he suddenly saw Bob, who said quickly:

"Good morning, Mr. Hughson. I trust you had a comfortable night after your adventures on the river."

"I don't know you, my lad," returned the man, with a broad accent, "and my name is not Hughson. I'm in a bit of a hurry, and—"

"Your name may not be Hughson, fast enough, but you are a British spy and we want you. You do know me, but I will refresh your memory a bit. I am Lieutenant Bob Estabrook of the Liberty Boys, and you were captured by us a night or two ago in the city."

"Never saw you in my life, and I am not a spy, but as good a rebel as yourself," and the man hurried to the barn at the rear of the house.

"You are not a patriot," said Bob, following. "We do not call ourselves rebels."

45

Then Bob imitated the crowing of a cock, and in a moment Dick came out and hurried forward. Hughson turned at the sound, saw Dick almost upon him, and whipped out a pistol. In an instant, however, Bob was upon him with a pistol at his head and his other hand on the spy's wrist.

Then Hughson suddenly found himself covered by a pistol in Dick's hand, the young captain saying:

"Take his weapon, Bob, and see if he has any others. Mr. Hughson, you are wanted in the city. Do you prefer going there dead or would you rather go alive?"

The man blanched, for he knew that he was in desperate straits and that his chances of escape were slight. He made a sudden dash, wrenching his hand free and attempted to fire at Dick, but Bob, by a quick thrusting out of his left foot, sent him upon his face on the grass. A man and a boy came running from the barn, and two housemaids appeared at the rear door shortly, followed by the landlord. Dick and Bob sprang forward and seized the man as he arose, holding him firmly.

"What is the trouble, Captain?" asked, the landlord, recognizing Dick, whom he had met before.

"We have caught a British spy, Boniface. He is a troublesome fellow and has already made his escape once."

"Bless my heart! A British spy, say you? Why, he told me he was a drover going into the city to get orders for cattle."

"And he told me he was a rebel," laughed Bob, "thus arousing my suspicions at once. We are not rebels and we do not recognize any."

"We call you rebels!" snarled the spy.

"But we do not," echoed Dick, "and if you were a better observer and consequently a better spy, you would have known it."

The others now came up and regarded the man with decided curiosity.

"The fellow had a horse, didn't he, Boniface?" asked Dick.

"Yes, he had, and a very good one."

"Will you have it brought out? We will lose no time in going back to the city."

"Yes, I will have it brought at once. Jenkins, get the drover's horse immediately."

"You will let me finish my pipe and pot, won't you?" asked the spy. "You took me rather by surprise."

"If you are not long over them," answered Dick.

Bob meanwhile, had deftly searched the man for concealed weapons and had taken them all away, so that Hughson might not cheat them by killing himself. He drank a pot of homebrew and puffed at his pipe under the trees, and then the groom announced that his horse was ready and he was quickly in the saddle. He said nothing as he rode away between the two boys, but seemed to be thinking deeply.

"You rebels don't have very much money," he said at last. "What would you consider a fair amount to allow me to escape?"

"You have made two serious errors," replied Dick coolly. "First, we are not rebels, as I have frequently told you, and second we are not for sale. Do you think we are as mean as yourself, who associate with thieves and murderers to gain your ends? There is not money enough in the world to induce us to violate our oaths."

"But why should you deliver me up to death, when I have never done you harm?"

"You forget last night," tersely. "Who tied me in a sack and threw me into the river?"

"Well, but I gave you a knife to—"

"You did not. That was Tom Fletcher. You had nothing to do with it. You came out upon the river in a boat afterward to look for me, fearing that I would escape. Don't add lying to your other faults."

The man rode on in silence for ten or fifteen minutes, and then suddenly said:

"You will be no better off if you do deliver me up to your rebel general, for Howe will be in possession of your wretched little city by tomorrow and the lot of you may be shot."

"If it is such a wretched little city, why does General Howe bother himself about it?" laughed Bob, Dick saying nothing.

"If you will let me go I will find a way for you to escape, and—"

"If you say another word on that subject I will gag you!" interrupted Dick sternly. "We are not to be bought, I tell you!"

Hughson flushed and remained silent after that, and at length the boys met some American soldiers and turned the spy over to them.

"That disposes of him," said Dick shortly.

"Yes, but he has been a very troublesome fellow, and would have been if we had not caught him. That was a very fortunate meeting."

"Except for him!" grimly.

"Very true, but, as Patsy says, we don't consider the enemy's feelings in such matters."

Returning to the camp, the boys heard from Mark that there had been considerable activity among the ships of the enemy during the afternoon, and that there were more at Governor's Island and one or two much nearer the mouth of the Hudson than during the morning.

"It is all very threatening," declared Dick, "and I think that the spy was right when he said that Howe will try to be in possession of the city by to-morrow. At the latest, it cannot be more than a day or two and then we must look out for ourselves."

"As we generally have to do!" laughed Bob.

CHAPTER X.–Caught in a Trap.

There was time enough before supper for Dick to visit the general, and shortly after his arrival in camp he went out afoot and made his way across the Commons and down Broadway. Seeing the general, Dick informed him of the capture of the spy, and what the man had said about Howe.

"It looks as if we might have trouble in a short time, Captain," the veteran answered, "and you will hold your Liberty Boys in readiness to act at a moment's notice at all times."

"I will do so, General," replied Dick. "If there is to be any fighting, the Liberty Boys will be glad to take part in it and do their share in opposing the advance of the enemy."

"I have always found them ready to do that, Captain," Putnam replied, "and to do it well, too. I have every confidence in you and the Liberty Boys, Captain, and I know that you will all do your best wherever you may be posted."

Dick then saluted and left the general, taking his way down to the lower end of the island in order to see for himself what was going on among the ships. On Whithall wharf he suddenly came face to face with Fletcher, Tom's father, the man being in a semi-intoxicated state at the time, and glaring fiercely at him as he said:

"You got away last night, you confounded rebel, but you don't do it again so easy. What have you done with my wife and the young ones? Nice business, ain't it, turning a wife against a husband?"

"You have turned her against you by your own outrageous conduct," Dick retorted. "If you had treated them right, your family would have remained with you, but you cannot expect anything better when you act as you have."

"Where have they gone? I have a right to everything that any of them earns, and I'm going to have it. Tom is under age, I have brought him up, and I can claim everything he has, and whatever my wife has also. I know my rights, I tell you!" savagely.

"Do you know your duties, as well?" sharply. "I don't care what the law is in your case. I know what justice is. You made an attempt upon my life last night, and if I choose to make a charge against you, I could put you on trial for your life."

The man was not so much intoxicated that he could not understand Dick's position and his own danger, and he turned pale and moved hurriedly away, losing himself in the crowd that thronged the wharf at the time.

"I don't think I shall have any more trouble from Mr. Fletcher," thought Dick, "or not on account of this affair, at any rate."

He remained on the wharf till nearly sunset, and then set out for the camp, where he arrived shortly before supper. There was an alarm during the night, and early the next morning Dick learned that some ships had passed up both rivers, and not long after this there was the sound of heavy firing at some distance above the city, and the boys knew that the enemy had succeeded in landing troops. There was great excitement in the city, and many of the inhabitants began leaving in great haste.

Dick hurried off to Putnam's quarters, and soon afterward word was received that the city was to be evacuated. The general despatched Dick to the lower part of the city to see that there were no ships coming up the river and to warn the men at the lower batteries to leave. Dick took Bob and a dozen or more of the boys with him and hurried away on foot, sending Mark and the rest of the boys toward the upper part of the island. The boys had performed a part of their mission and were returning, when they suddenly heard a great bombarding from the river and at the same time saw a considerable body of redcoats coming toward them.

"To the stone house, boys!" hissed Dick. "These fellows know nothing of it and we are safe there."

The stone house was the nearest place of refuge, and the boys hurried to it, the redcoats losing sight of them. They reached the place in safety, and were all inside and out of sight before the redcoats came to the wharf and began to look for them. The door above was closed and looked as if it had not been open in months, the boys not having been seen to enter it. Dick and Bob hurried below, leaving Ben, Harry, Sam and others at the upper door, while the rest scattered through the building. There were a few persons on the wharf below when the redcoats came along, but these had not seen the boys and knew nothing about them.

"What place is that?" asked a sergeant of redcoats of one of the loungers, pointing to the stone house.

"Just an old warehouse," the man answered.

"Is there any one in it?"

"No, not now," was the reply.

Dick was listening at the door, and he knew the man to be one of the rascals who had been in the house but had escaped. There was a reason, therefore, for the man not saying very much about the place.

"Why not?" the sergeant asked.

"Because the rebels arrested 'em and took all the stuff out," the man replied.

"We shall have to get a look at the place," the redcoat said, and he promptly went to the door with a dozen of his men.

The door was locked and was very strong, and the sergeant speedily came to the conclusion that there was little use in trying to force it and so gave up the attempt.

"Have you seen any rebels about here?" he asked, but the other man was gone, and those he spoke to said:

"No, there hain't been nobody here sence we come around."

The sergeant and the redcoats, as well as a second lieutenant and another party, examined the region all about the place, but saw nothing of the boys and so concluded that they had gone elsewhere. There was a guard of about a dozen left on the wharf, but none on the bank above, the rest going into the city. The loungers about the place, evidently fearing that they might be pressed into the service, went away, and thus there was no one to give any information to the redcoats, which might have resulted in giving the house another visit.

Dick sent Harry and Will to the cellar and thence under the wharf to the river, the boys reporting that the tide was high and that there was no getting out that way at that time. Then one of the boys was sent to the upper door to keep a lookout, Dick going to see him in a few minutes.

"There are redcoats on the Commons, Captain," the boy reported. "A couple of men went by here just now and I heard them talking about it."

"We can leave the house," remarked Dick, "but we would not get a great way before being discovered, and I think it better we remain here for a time, till dark, perhaps."

"We are caught in a trap," muttered Bob, "but the redcoats don't know it, and that's the only hopeful thing about it."

"We are not caught in a trap exactly, Bob," declared Dick. "Say, rather, that we are hiding from them, and that as soon as we see a good chance we are coming out and will make a run for it."

"And in the meantime what are we going to do for something to eat and drink?" asked Bob.

"We may find something in the house, but we shall have to take it cold, for as soon as we start a fire we will excite suspicion."

"I found some old clothes in one of the rooms, Captain," said Ben, "and when the coast is a bit clear some of us can go out and get food. I will go, for one."

"Very good, Ben, but not now," replied Dick.

Later, when there was no one about the upper floor, Dick, Ben and Harry went out, looking like three vagabonds, and looked about them. Dick went toward the Commons, and Ben and Harry took their way toward the church to get some food. There were redcoats on the Commons, as Dick had feared, and he could see more of them in the distance. Then he walked carelessly on, seeing no one who knew him, and made his way as far as a quiet inn down a side street where he was well known, the people being good patriots. On the way he saw many redcoats, Hessians, and other enemies, and he knew that getting out of New York was going to be a difficult task, and one that would require all their energy as well as a deal of craft and caution.

"What, you are still in the city, Captain?" asked the landlord, when he recognized Dick.

"Yes, there are nearly a score of us who were caught here, but I hope to get away to-night."

"There are lines drawn right across the city and island, and the redcoats will let no one through whom they do not know."

"There is the river," added Dick. "We are in the old warehouse down there, and if we can get a boat or two we will try to get out of the city that way."

"There are ships in the river, Captain, that are keeping a sharp lookout. I don't want to discourage you, but I am afraid that it will be as hard to get out that way as any."

"I am glad to know all the difficulties there are in our way, for then I shall know how to meet them. It is better to know just what to expect."

"Of course, and I will give you all the help I can."

"Thank you. If I need it, I will call on you."

CHAPTER XI.–Getting Away Under Difficulties.

Dick secured a basketful of food to take to the boys, knowing that Ben and Harry would procure more, and therefore not taking any more than he could conveniently carry without arousing suspicion. The city was full of redcoats, and at every step he realized the danger he ran, and also that it would increase with every hour that he and the boys remained in New York.

"We must get out to-night as soon as we can procure boats," he said to himself, "There must be some way of getting them, and we must have them, as they are absolutely necessary."

He returned to the stone house, getting in by the lower door without being observed, the other boys returning shortly afterward by the upper entrance.

"It will be difficult to get away by any of the regular roads," declared Ben, "and even if we all had disguises, it is going to be a difficult matter to pass the guard."

"I was thinking of getting out of New York by way of the river, Ben," said Dick.

"That will be something less difficult, though hard enough, but where are we going to get our boats?"

"There are ships in the river not very far away, and it may be that they will anchor still nearer. The men will want to come ashore and we must get hold of at least two boats. I don't think one will be sufficient, even if it is a long boat. Watch the river, boys, and see what are our chances."

The boys ate some of the food which Dick and the rest had procured, and while some rested, others kept a lookout on the river, on the wharf and on the bank above. At times the paths were well frequented, and men and women could be seen on the walk above, the wharf being now quite busy and then almost deserted, although at no time would it have been wise for the boys in uniform to have ventured out. Well on in the afternoon a ship came up the river and anchored right off the stone house, well out in the stream, another being something above it.

"The bluejackets will be coming ashore some time in the evening to enjoy themselves," remarked Dick. "It will be high tide, and if we can get hold of the boat, we can perhaps hide it under the wharf."

"Unless it is too high," said Bob. "The tides are pretty heavy just now."

"Then we can leave from the wharf itself, but we shall have to do everything with despatch, for it is likely that a watch will be kept on the river and along shore, and the least suspicious act will bring down the night patrol and the watch, as well as the redcoats and sailors."

"No good thing can be had without effort," said Bob dryly, "and if we want our freedom we must work for it."

It was after dark when two boats came ashore from the nearest vessel and tied up at the wharf a short distance from the stone house. The sailors went ashore, leaving the boats without any one to look after them, but there were men on the wharf and constant passing to and fro of men and boys.

"We shall have to wait a while," said Dick. "When it is quieter there will be more chance to secure the boats."

"Then it may be too late," muttered Bob, "for the sailors will be going back to the ship."

"They will not return till late, for no sailor wants to cut short his shore leave."

"There may be a few minutes when all is quiet, and in the interim we can make a run for the boats and get away."

"Yes, and we must be on the lookout for just such a time."

The boys waited patiently, but it seemed as if no one wanted to go to bed, and as if there would be something going on all night. Finally, realizing the danger of waiting too long, Dick said to Bob and some of the boys:

"I am going to make my way to the other end of the wharf and get up some sort of disturbance to draw the people away from the boats. You must take that opportunity to seize them and get away. Then I will join you and we will all leave."

"You won't get caught?" asked Bob. "If I thought there was any danger, I would insist on going with you."

"There will be danger, of course, but I will take care of myself."

"I don't think that it will be wise to have too many of us away from the boats."

"No, perhaps not."

Dick shortly crept out cautiously by the lower door, having a long coat over his uniform, and made his way toward the farther end of the wharf and get up some sort of disturbance to draw the people away from the boats. "You must take that opportunity to seize them and get away. Then I will join you and we will all leave."

"You won't get caught?" asked Bob. "If I thought there was any danger, I would insist on going with you."

"There will be danger, of course, but I will take care of myself."

"I don't think that it will be wise to have too many of us away from the boats."

"No, perhaps not."

Dick shortly crept out cautiously by the lower door, having a long coat over his uniform, and made his way toward the farther end of the wharf. The boys were to act as soon as they heard any unusual noise from his direction, Bob taking the lead. Making his way along the wharf, Dick presently saw a nightwatch with a lantern at the end of a long pole coming toward them.

"Here is the watch," said one, "come to send us to bed."

"Let us put out his lantern and souse him in the river," said Dick, with a laugh.

"That's so, that will be great fun."

A man with a lantern came up at this moment and the light fell upon Dick.

"Hallo! if there isn't the rebel!" the man shouted.

The fellow was Tom's father, Dick recognizing him at that moment. Here was the chance to create the disturbance, and Dick at once sprang at the man, knocked him down, and said:

"Take that, you sot! We will see if you can insult honest folks for nothing!"

At once there was a shout, and some of the man's friends sprang at Dick with shouts and a great uproar. In the scuffle Dick lost his long coat, letting it go rather than be seized by one of the thieves. The night watch and a number of redcoats were now seen coming on at a run.

"By George! the fellow is a rebel, after all! See his uniform."

"My word, that's Dick Slater himself! Seize him, there is a big reward offered for him."

Dick knocked down two of the crowd and pushed another into the water from the wharf. There was a great outcry, and now men and boys began coming from all quarters to see the fight. The watch and the redcoats saw Dick and hurried forward to arrest him as a rebel and for creating a disturbance. The people, fearing to be apprehended by the watch, hurried away by this and that way of escape, and Dick had a clear coast. Then he gave a signal which told the boys to get away as quickly as possible. They had already seized the two boats and filled them rapidly.

"Take in Dick, boys," said Bob, heading one of the boats, "while I go ahead to clear the way."

Harry, Ben, Sam, Phil and others were in the other boat, which lay alongside the wharf, ready to take Dick on board. Meanwhile the alarm was spreading that Dick Slater, the captain of the Liberty Boys, was in the city and that whoever would seize him would receive a large reward. Dick, close pressed, sounded a signal to the boys to get away at once for fear of being caught. It were better that he were taken, he reasoned, than that all the boys should be made prisoners. Bob, in his boat, thinking that Dick was all right, went on out upon the river. Redcoats, nightwatch, sailors and populace joined in the pursuit, pressing the young patriot sorely. He had to dodge and take a longer course to the boat in order to reach it at all and then signalled to the boys to go on. Harry and his boys, supposing that Dick had in some way reached the other boat, took up their oars and began to pull. Then Dick found a way suddenly to dart between two of the redcoats and run rapidly toward the water. There was a great outcry and the chase waxed hotter than ever. The redcoats and the nightwatch pursued Dick to the very edge of the wharf.

The boat containing the Liberty Boys was just putting out. Dick jumped and was caught by Harry. The redcoats were too late. A furious captain, in his haste to seize Dick rushed forward with drawn sword, and in a moment went pitching headlong, and was speedily seen floundering in the water, his wig floating in one direction and his hat in another, his sword sinking to the bottom, as he was suddenly forced to swim for it or go down. The nightwatch lost his lantern in the scuffle, and there was great confusion and hubbub. In the dark, men behind pushing forward to see what was going on crowded redcoats and others into the river, and the confusion and hubbub grew worse and worse every moment.

"Hallo, keep back there, you are throwing us all into the river!"

"Good thing, too, to get rid of all the redcoats!"

"Push a few more in and give them a good soaking."

"Shove in a few rebels to even things up."

"What's all the trouble about, anyhow?"

"Ten o'clock of a sultry night and all's well!" drawled the nightwatch, recovering his lantern and lighting it.

Then other nightwatchmen came up, and there was more light and less confusion and turmoil. The redcoats were very wroth at the people for letting the "saucy young rebels" escape, and the bluejackets were angry at the rebels for taking their boats, while some of the people were wrathful at both redcoats and bluejackets, and others,–Tories, by the way–were incensed against the others and angry at the escape of the boys.

The latter were now out upon the river in the dark, but going cautiously and steadily on. Dick took the lead and worked his way between the shore and the nearest ship without being discovered, the hubbub on shore not having yet resolved itself into an alarm which the ships could understand. The officers, supposing it to be merely a fight between rival crews or between sailors and people, paid no attention to it, and the boys continued steadily on their way. Then other boats put out, and some one shouted:

"Hallo! there's a boatload of young rebels on the river, trying to escape. Fire upon them and sink the young rascals the moment you see them!"

Now the cause of the fracas on shore was explained, and at once a search for the daring boys was instituted. Lights flashed, hoarse voices were heard calling across the water, and there was as much confusion on the river as there had been on land. One could not see as far as on shore, however, and the means of getting from place to place were not as numerous, and much time was lost in getting into communication one with another.

Dick knew his way and went on as rapidly as possible, and with all caution, passing one ship and making his way toward the next. In the dark, the blue uniforms of the boys could easily be mistaken for the blue jackets or sailors or midshipmen, and Dick relied upon this to help him in his escape. A boat had been lowered, and presently the sound of the boys' oars was heard by the enemy.

"Ahoy! What boat is that?"

"Seen anything of the rebels, sir?" asked Dick, the boys pulling steadily.

"No, not yet. Have you?"

"I've an idea there's a boatload of them ahead of us somewhere, but it's dark as Erebus on the river."

"Go ahead and keep a watch. My idea is that they have not gone as far as this yet."

"An idea that you are quite welcome to, my man!" was Dick's thought. "Everybody thinks that his idea is the only correct one."

Bob was hailed by the other boat as he followed Dick closely, and answered gruffly:

"Port, captain! Keep a watch below there, and keep a sharper eye on your duty. The rebels may have gone down the river, for all you know. There is no good in looking one way only."

"Aye, aye, sir!" and the boat went down the river.

The ship was passed in safety, the boats being supposed to be filled with middies and bluejackets, and no questions were asked. There were dangers ahead of the boys, however, and they all realized that running the blockade was not going to be as easy a matter as one might think.

CHAPTER XII.–On the River.

There were other ships up the river, and there were the chevaux-de-frise which the patriots had constructed to keep the enemy out, and which would now be a hindrance to the boys. They must get beyond the ships and the obstructions before dawn, or they would be captured, and they all realized the dangers to be met. It was better for the two boats to keep together, but in case they were beset, it might be wiser for them to separate and the boys understood this. They had passed the ships nearest to their hiding place, and unless the alarm spread to those farther up the river, it might not be so hard to pass these also.

The alarm might be carried alongshore, however, and there might be boats out watching for parties of patriots trying to get over to the Jersey shore, and all these things must be taken into consideration in pushing forward. The boys rowed steadily, all of them being accustomed to being on the water, and their progress was steady if not very rapid, it being dark on the river, and the current and the tide being both against them.

Rowing on steadily, they at length heard sounds behind them, which told them that the search below had been thorough, and that the enemy were convinced that they had gone up the river instead of down, and the pursuit was now being carried on in that direction. A bright light was seen from the masthead of a ship below them, this being meant as a signal to those above. As they went on, they saw a light flash from the masthead of a vessel some way ahead of them.

"Pull steady, boys," he said. "We may be able to pass the ship without being seen, and, if not, I think I can find a way to fool them and run the blockade."

As they went on, a boat was seen crossing their bow at some little distance, and Dick told the boys to get the lanterns ready. On they went, and at last a hail came from the boat ahead:

"Ahoy! Who are you?"

The lanterns suddenly flashed, and Dick cried:

"There are the rebels, men. Don't let them fool you. Get ready, all of you!"

"Hello! Boat ahoy! Are you looking for rebels?"

"Yes, and we've got you! Surrender, or we'll run you down!"

"Why, you dunderhead, we are looking for rebels ourselves!"

"By George! then they must be below. Go down there and look for them!"

"What authority have you over us, I'd like to know?" in an angry tone.

"See that masthead light? That means to look out for the enemy. We are here to see that the enemy are looked out for. That's my authority! Pull ahead, my men!"

The middy in the other boat saw just enough blue and gold lace to mistake Dick for a naval officer, and the young patriot's tone of authority did the rest.

"Very good, sir!" promptly, and the boats containing the boys went on, the names painted on the sterns being seen, and no one supposing that any one but British bluejackets would be in them.

"Keep a sharp lookout below there, Midshipman!" said Dick, in a commanding tone. "There is no use of that light. You are only giving the rebels warning."

The other boat went on, and the masthead light was presently extinguished, much to Bob's delight.

"The thing has burned out, I suppose," he muttered, "and they will not renew it. Good thing, too!"

"Keep on steady, boys, and make as little noise as possible," said Dick. "We are not out of danger yet, and no one knows what may happen before we get up to the obstructions."

"We may be able to go ashore there, Captain," observed Harry, "in place of having to get through them."

"Yes, if there are no lines drawn across the island at that point. We can tell better when we get there."

It was all dark on the river again in a few minutes, and the two boats keeping close together proceeded steadily on, making very fair progress.

"Would it be of any advantage to make our way over to the Jersey shore and cross again higher up the river, Dick?" asked Bob.

"I am not sure that it would, Bob," was the reply. "We will not do it unless we have to, as we can probably make better time by keeping on as we are."

The day had been sultry, but it was now cold and damp on the river, being dark as well, a cold mist arising as they went on, which not only made it more difficult to see their way but chilled them as well. However, if they could not see the enemy, the latter could not see them, so that there was an advantage on their side after all. They went as far as Bloomingdale without seeing anything of the enemy or hearing any alarm, and were in hope of going the rest of the way safely, when the mist lifted for a few moments, and Dick saw the outlines of a ship looming up before him out of the darkness. He quickly steered out of the day and signalled to Bob to go closer inshore so as to avoid the ship. Presently a light appeared on board, and then a voice called out in sharp tones:

"Boat ahoy! What are you doing out there?"

"Looking out for the enemy!" answered Dick, that being just what he was doing.

"Seen anything of them?"

"Yes, some little time ago. Seen any yourselves?"

"No, what are they up to? Sending out their confounded fireboats to annoy us?"

"Oh, they'll do anything, I fancy," and the boats went on, the men on the ships never imagining that they contained a number of the Liberty Boys.

"Keep a good watch for them, and if you see any give us a signal."

"Aye, aye! we'll keep a strict watch for them."

"That's what we've been doing ever since we left New York," muttered Ben, under his breath.

The ship was presently lost in the mist and darkness, and the boys went on, not knowing when they might come upon another. They kept close together, so as not to be separated, and drew as near to the shore as was safe, the ships being mostly in midstream. Now and then the darkness was so dense as to shut out everything, and once they ran upon a bar and had to push themselves off with considerable exertion, being unable to see anything. Getting off at last, they went on, but were at length hailed by a boat out on the river and not far from them.

"Boat ahoy!" cried Dick, in answer to the hail. "Are you from the Royal George?"

"No, the Inflexible. Are you from the George?"

"No; we are looking for her. We are carrying despatches."

"She must be up the river. We have seen nothing of her. Who are you?"

"Despatch boat. Keep a sharp lookout for the enemy. They are getting troublesome."

"Aye, aye!" and Dick and his boys went on rapidly, getting farther and farther away from the other boat every minute.

"The river is full of the pesky British!" muttered Bob. "I am not sure that it would not be safer to go ashore."

"We are sure of our road here, Bob," laughed Dick, "but we would not be, on shore. I think we had better stick to the river for a time, until dawn, at any rate."

"H'm! it can't be far from it, then, for I never knew it to be thundering dark," growled Bob.

The boys laughed and went on less rapidly, that being the safest course. They took turns rowing, and so no one became over-fatigued and all had a chance to warm up, the mists of the river being very chilly and damp. At length it grew light enough to see the obstructions in the river just ahead of them, and they set about getting through and going on. Dick would have gone ashore, but he saw tents and the gleam of scarlet uniforms on shore, and concluded that it would be better to remain longer on the river. The boats had much less trouble in getting past the obstructions than a ship would have had, and they got through at length, with some trouble, being seen by the redcoats on shore, however, it being very much lighter by this time.

The enemy raised a great shout, but they had no boats, and all they could do was to run along shore and shout, firing a volley now and then, which did no damage and only set the echoes to answering.

"They had better keep quiet," sputtered Bob. "The first thing we know they will wake up everybody along shore, and we will have some trouble in making a landing."

"I think we might do it before long, Bob," Dick returned. "A run will do us good after being on the river so many hours."

"All right, Dick, and if we can give the redcoats a run the right way, so much the better."

Farther on, around a bend of the river, the redcoats being now out of sight, the boys rowed in to shore and made a landing. They had left their muskets behind, but they all had their pistols and were ready to give the redcoats as lively a reception as they could. The boats were left to go adrift, and then, led by Dick, who knew the way thoroughly, they set out for their own lines, which Dick judged would be somewhere below Fort Washington. On they went, and all at once came upon a party of the enemy hurrying to intercept them.

"Fire, Liberty Boys!" shouted Dick. "Scatter the redcoats, drive them off the island, hurl them into the river!"

"Liberty forever, forward, down with the redcoats!" echoed the plucky fellows.

Then they began to discharge their pistols in the liveliest fashion, and to shout as if there were four or five times as many of them. The redcoats evidently thought that there were many more of the daring boys, and fell back in haste. Dick and Bob led the way, and the whole party charged resolutely, desiring to get to a place of safety as soon as possible, although it seemed to the enemy as if they were being pursued by an army, and they made all haste to get away.

The boys turned up the road toward the fort with all haste, and were well on their way before the enemy realized that they were not being pursued. Then they turned and went after the boys, greatly chagrined at having been so cleverly fooled. They got reinforcements, and set out after the boys in full chase, but were suddenly brought to a stop by the main body of the Liberty Boys under Mark Morrison. Mark had heard the firing, and was out looking for Dick and the Liberty Boys at the same time, and now, seeing their danger, fell upon the enemy tooth and nail and sent them flying.

"Hurrah! back with the redcoats!" he shouted. "Give it to them, my boys. Fire!"

Crash–roar! The redcoats now had to face a musket volley instead of a pistol discharge, and they felt the difference. Down upon them bore the gallant boys with a cheer and a ringing volley, and then two or three brigades of regulars were seen following up the boys, and they fell back in great disorder.

"Hurrah!" yelled Bob. "That's the kind of reception to get. Here we are, boys!"

CHAPTER XIII.–Tom Joins the Liberty Boys.

Mark and his boys gave Dick and Bob and the rest a hearty cheer, and then the whole body took a stand to be ready to meet the enemy in case they should make another advance. The patriots were out in full force now, however, and the redcoats fell back to the edge of Harlem Plains, where they had their camp, the plan being a sort of neutral ground between the two armies.

The boys shortly retired to their own camp, and here Dick and Bob and Ben, and the rest who had been left in the city, were given a right royal welcome, and then they all had breakfast together, Dick and his boys being very glad to get it. Mark and the others were eager to hear what had befallen them in the city, and were greatly interested in hearing the story of their many and varied adventures. "We had some trouble ourselves in getting away," declared Mark, "but nothing like what you fellows had. You must have given the redcoats a good scare at times, however."

"It was the only chance we had of getting away," laughed Bob. "If we had not made them think we were ten times as strong as we were, we would have been gobbled up."

The enemy made one or two sorties during the day, but were in every case driven back, and at last retired to their lines and did not again seek to molest the Americans. The patriots had lost New York, but they were still in possession of the upper part of the island and meant to hold it as long as they could, Fort Washington being a strong fort and well defended. At night the Liberty Boys' camp was well guarded, and the slightest move of the enemy toward it would have been detected in a moment. During the forenoon, Tom came to the camp and said:

"It's a fine place where we are, Captain, and I am obliged to you for sending us up there. Mother will get plenty to do and already has the promise of enough to keep her busy for a month."

"I am very glad of it, Tom," said Dick, "and I am sure that you will all be much happier there than in the city. The enemy are there now, and it will be much worse than before."

"So the redcoats have gone into New York, have they? I am sorry for that."

"So are we all, Tom, but it will not be forever. Some day we will be back there again, and the British will be driven out and have to go back to their own country beyond the sea."

"The sooner the better!" muttered Tom.

"Tell them when you go back that we are all right, Tom," Dick resumed. "Some of us had a hard time getting out of New York and had to run the blockade, but we got out fast enough and gave the redcoats some pretty good slaps."

"The young ladies will be glad to hear of it. Did you see him again, Captain?"

"Yes, and he made some trouble for us, but we got away all right for all of him, and I doubt if we shall ever see him again."

"Well, I hope not, but you can't tell. What you don't expect is just what happens."

"At all events, he has no idea that you and your mother are up here, Tom, and it is not likely that he will trouble you any more."

"Well, I hope he won't, Captain, but you can't tell, as I said."

"No, but we will do all we can to keep him away. His reputation is not good, and if he appears in camp we will warn him that if he does not keep away he will be arrested."

"That may have some effect, though if he thought that arresting just meant being put in jail he wouldn't care, because he's been there before lots of times."

"We will make him understand just what it means, Tom," said Dick, "and I think he will keep away, but then, he has not appeared at all yet."

"No, that's so, and I was making out as if he had or was going to," with a smile. "Well, perhaps he won't."

The boy's look and tone seemed to indicate that he was afraid the man would come, however, and Dick said no more about it. Tom went back to Dick's house, and the Liberty Boys did not see him again for two or three days. Meantime the commander-in-chief, whose confidence Dick enjoyed, sent for the boy and said:

"There is an important mission which I wish to entrust to some one, Captain, and I know of no better, person than yourself to do it. Get ready at once to go down to the city and obtain certain information. Procure a disguise and a horse, and then come to me, and I will furnish you with money for your expenses and a pass, which will enable you to get through the lines."

"Very good, your excellency," Dick replied, and in half an hour he was ready to start.

Bob, Mark, or any of the Liberty Boys, in fact, would have been glad to go with him, but the general thought it was best to go alone, and so he took no one with him. The pass had been taken from a spy whom the patriots had captured and enabled Dick to get through the lines in safety. Reaching the city, he set about getting the information required, and secured it the first day he was there. That night there was an alarm of fire in the lower part of the city, and Dick dressed himself and went out with many others to ascertain its extent and see what he could do to help put it down.

It had started in a low groggery on Whitehall wharf and was of considerable extent, spreading as far as Beaver street, and then shifting to the west, and going as far as the river and nearly to Partition street, Trinity church being destroyed on the way. It had started by accident, but many of the British declared that it had been set by the Americans, and there was a bitter feeling against them, many innocent persons being put to death by the enraged people.

During the fire, while Dick was working with others to stop its spreading, a man was caught looting a burning house and was at once dragged away and hanged to a post holding a street lamp. Dick saw his face for an instant and recognized Tom's father. There was no interceding for the man, who had been caught red-handed, and he suffered the penalty of his crimes.

"His wife and the rest are the better off for his taking away," said Dick to himself, "but I cannot tell how he died. He was never of any use to them and they are better off without him."

The fire burned out at length, but there were smoking ruins the next day and for several days, although Dick did not remain as long as that. He got away the next day and made his way out of the city and to the camp with very little difficulty, his pass being of great assistance to him. Changing his clothes and putting on his uniform, Dick reported at once to the commander-in-chief and was complimented upon securing the information so promptly. Reporting other matters that he had learned, Dick returned to the camp and told Bob and a few others how the Tory had met his death, adding:

"Do not say anything to Tom about it. I will tell him that his father is dead, but not how it happened. It is a hard thing to say, perhaps, but they are better off without him than they ever were with him."

"It is the truth, at any rate," muttered Bob, "though it may not be necessary to tell them."

A few days later the Liberty Boys were ordered into lower Westchester to check the advance of Howe and Cornwallis, who were trying to get behind the Americans at King's Bridge and thus have a better opportunity to attack Fort Washington, which the British leader had set his heart upon subduing.

"That will give us plenty to do," declared Bob, "and give us a chance to bother the redcoats."

"And give Patsy a chance to get rid of some of his extra fat," laughed Mark, who was a bit of a tease.

"Sure Oi've none to spare at all, Liftinant," roared Patsy, "but if ye had said Cookyspiller now, ye'd have hit it to a tay. Sure he do be nadin' it had."

As the boys were getting ready to leave, Tom came into camp and said:

"So you are leaving, are you, Captain? You have not seen him, have you?"

"You will not see him again, Tom," Dick replied. "He was killed a few days ago while in the commission of a crime in the city."

"Did you see it, Captain?"

"Yes, Tom. You and your mother are now free."

Tom asked no questions, but presently said:

"I would like to join the Liberty Boys. Mother is doing very well, the little children are being cared for, and there is a good man up at Tarrytown who has lost his wife and needs some one to take care of his children. Mother can do it, and I think—"

"She will marry him in time, Tom? Yes, it will be good for both of them. She likes him?"

"Yes, and so do all of us. Is it wrong for me to think that we are better off now that he has been taken away?"

"You need not think anything about it, Tom, but you are better off, for all that. The man was simply a clog about the necks of all of you."

"Then I may join the Liberty Boys, if I am big enough? Mother does not need me now and I want to do something for my country."

"Your mother is willing, Tom?"

"Yes, if you will take me."

"Very good. You are young, but not too young, and you are strong and willing, and that is a good deal. I will see your mother, Tom, and I do not think there will be any trouble about your joining."

Tom returned to his mother and in a day or so Dick saw her and found that she was willing that Tom should join the company. Tom went back with Dick, therefore, and was sworn in as one of the Liberty Boys, to his great delight. The boys cheered him for they had all heard of him and knew of his sterling character and manly qualities. He fought with the Liberty Boys at White Plains and Fort Washington and went into the Jerseys with the troop when they joined the commander after the fall of the fort. He was at Trenton and Princeton, where he did brave work with the boys and fought through the succeeding campaign, doing good service at Brandywine and Germantown and going into camp at Valley Forge, where he bore with fortitude all the hardships of that rigorous winter, one of the severest ever known. During the next spring he was with the Liberty Boys in Connecticut and lost his life during a fight with Tryon's raiders. His mother had married in the meantime and was in comfortable circumstances, and this was a great comfort to the boy, who said to Dick:

"I have done my duty, Captain?"

"Yes, Tom, and well."

"And mother and the children are well and happy?"

"Yes, they are, Tom."

"We are sure to win this fight for freedom, Captain?"

"Yes, Tom, we cannot do otherwise."

"Then I have not died in vain in giving my life for my country?"

"No, Tom, you have not."

"Then I have nothing to regret. Good-by, Captain. You have been very good to me."

Dick took the boy's hand and held it till the grip relaxed, when he placed it at his side and spread the flag over the young hero.

Next week's issue will contain "THE LIBERTY BOYS AND CAPTAIN HUCK; or, ROUTING A WICKED LEADER."

A reporter was interviewing Thomas A. Edison. "And you, sir," he said to the inventor, "made the first talking machine?" "No," Mr. Edison replied, "the first one was made long before my time–out of a rib."

THE LIBERTY BOYS OF '76

— — LATEST ISSUES — —

1084	"	Hidden Swamp: or, Hot Times Along the Shore.
1085	"	and the Black Horseman; or, Defeating a Dangerous Foe.
1086	"	After the Cherokees; or, Battling With Cruel Enemies.
1087	"	River Journey; or, Down the Ohio.
1088	"	at East Rock; or, The Burning of New Haven.
1089	"	in the Drowned Lands; or, Perilous Times Out West.
1090	"	on the Commons; or, Defending Old New York.
1091	"	Sword Charge; or, The Fight at Stony Point.
1092	"	After Sir John; or, Dick Slater's Clever Ruse.
1093	"	Doing Guard Duty; or, The Loss of Fort Washington.
1094	"	Chasing a Renegade; or, The Worst Man on the Ohio.
1095	"	and the Fortune Teller; or, The Gypsy Spy of Harlem.
1096	"	Guarding Washington, or, Defeating a British Plot.
1097	"	and Major Davie; or, Warm Work in the Mecklenburg District.
1098	"	Fierce Hunt; or, Capturing a Clever Enemy.
1099	"	Betrayed; or, Dick Sister's False Friend.
1100	"	on the March: or, After a Slippery Foe.
1101	"	Winter Camp; or, Lively Times in the North.
1102	"	Avenged; or, The Traitor's Doom.
1103	"	Pitched Battle; or, The Escape of the Indian Spy.
1104	"	Light Artillery; or, Good Work At the Guns.
1105	"	and "Whistling Will"; or, The Mad Spy of Paulus Hook.
1106	"	Underground Camp; or, In Strange Quarters.
1107	"	Dandy Spy; or, Deceiving the Governor.